This book is dedicated to all the siblings out there,
but especially to my big brothers, Brooks and Mike

Balzer + Bray is an imprint of HarperCollins Publishers.

Confiscated!

ISBN 978-0-06-241086-3

The artist used mixed media, collage, and Photoshop to create the digital illustrations for this book.
Typography by Ellice M. Lee
16 17 18 19 20 SCP 10 9 8 7 6 5 4 3 2 1

First Edition

CONFISCATED!

Suzanne Kaufman

BALZER + BRAY
An Imprint of HarperCollinsPublishers

Brooks and Mikey fought over
EVERYTHING and ANYTHING.
And whenever they did, their
mama would take it away.

In other words, it got

CONFISCATED!

They fought over the bike.

Confiscated!

They fought over Grandpa's tuba.

CONFISCATED!

They fought over

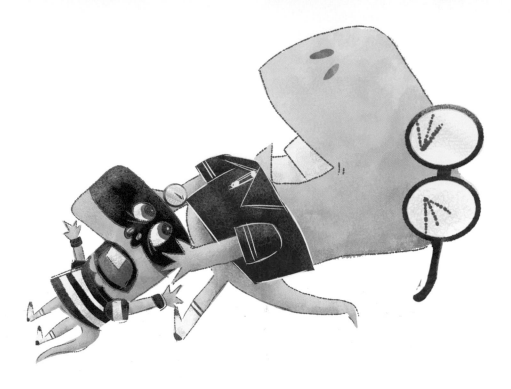

a Mexican wrestling mask,

the lightning-bolt cape,

Mikey's favorite car,

and Brooks's favorite stuffed animal.

Even the family dog wasn't safe.

They fought until Mama had confiscated
ALL their toys.

A Jurassic second later,
Brooks and Mikey were bored.

After a few more minutes,
they were really, REALLY bored.

There was nothing left to do but talk to each other.

"Yeah! And when we beat the Raptors at basketball

and rocked the talent show?"

"And remember when we won the last red balloon?"

Then they had an idea.
A really, really, REALLY good idea.

They lifted.

They stacked.

They climbed.

And they pulled . . . .

until out popped
that red balloon!

YES!

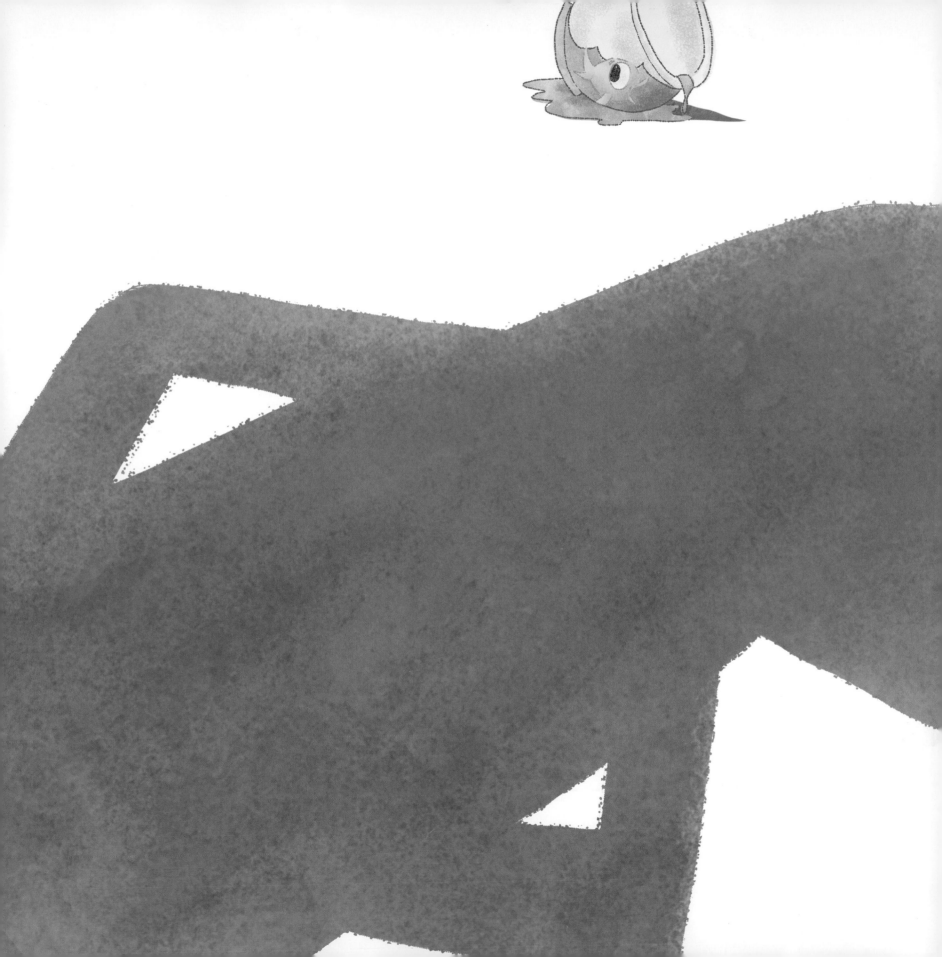

they got
BUSTED!

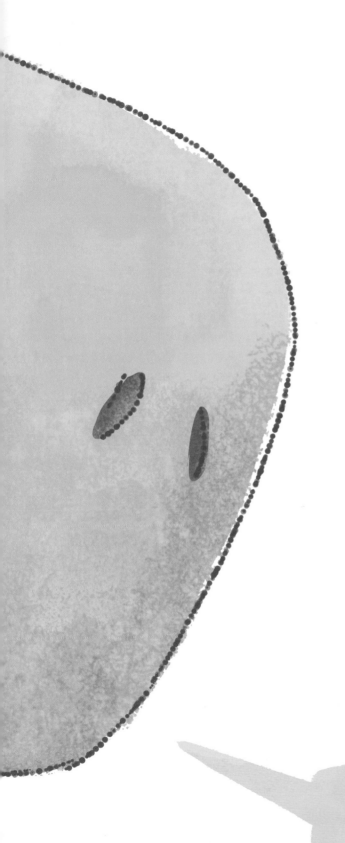

But Mama wasn't as angry as the boys expected.

Are you SHARING that balloon?

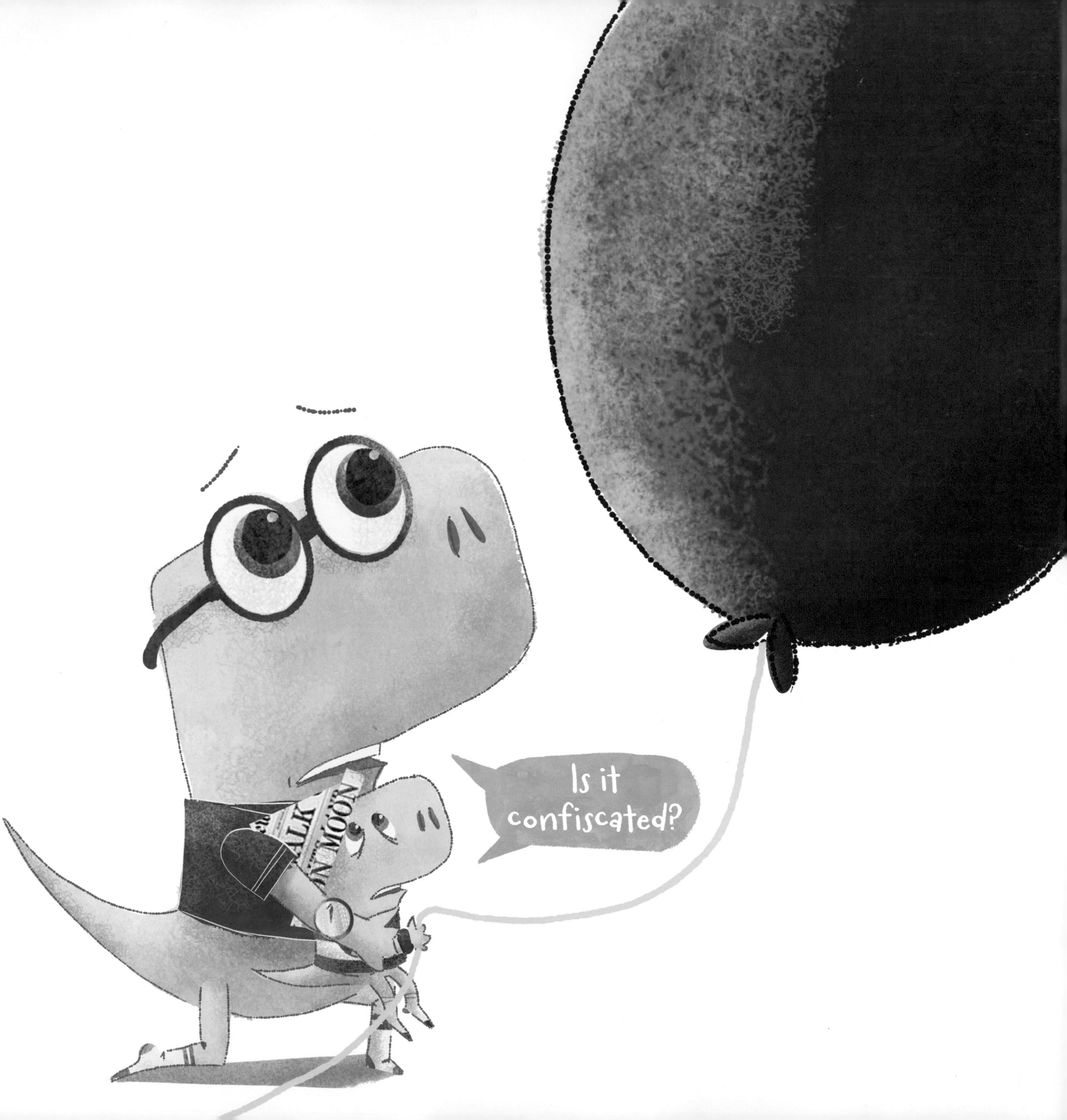
Is it confiscated?